The Perfect Little Monster

Judy Hindley   illustrated by **Jonathan Lycett-Smith**

CANDLEWICK PRESS
CAMBRIDGE, MASSACHUSETTS

Once there was a perfect little baby monster.
He had **horrible** little eyes and
a **horrible** little nose and
as soon as he was born,
he scowled.

His
family
loved him.

Baby Monster yelled and howled and made a **terrible** racket.

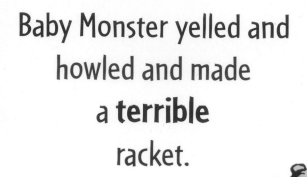

He threw his rattle and broke his bowl and made a **terrible** mess.

"Isn't he a perfect little monster!"
bragged his parents.

His sister taught him
how to **sneer**
and **snarl**.

His brother showed him
how to **bash** things
and **trash** things.

"Baby Monster learns so quickly!"
his parents said.

For his first birthday party,
Baby Monster's proud parents
invited all the monster aunts
and all the monster uncles and
all the many **horrible**
monster cousins.

Everyone gathered
around Baby Monster.
"Give us a great big scowl!"
said his mother
and father.

Baby Monster twitched his **horrible** little nose.

He scrunched up his **horrible** little eyes.

He opened his
horrible
little
mouth

and stretched his
horrible
little
lips.

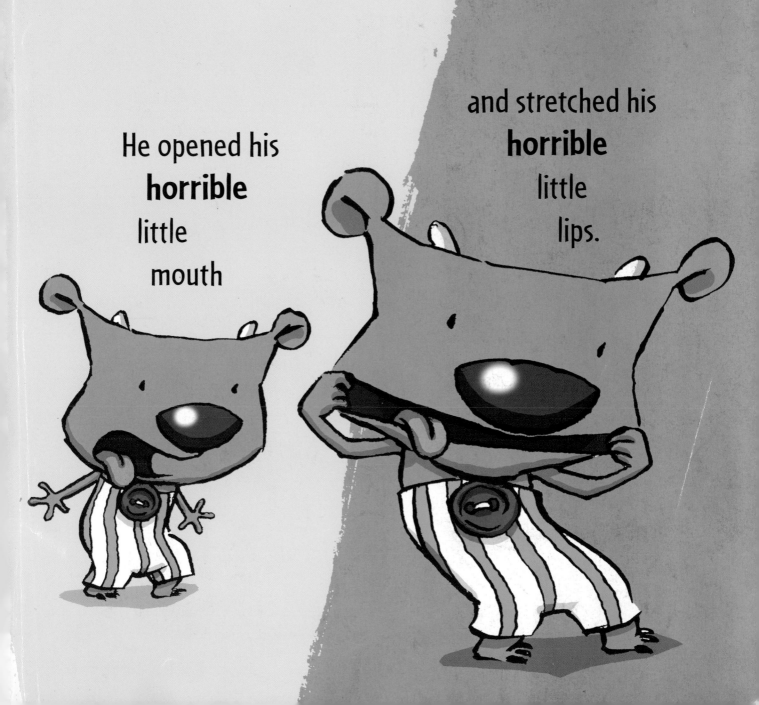

"No-no-no!" howled Mother and Father Monster.

"Ugh!" cried Sister Monster.

"YUCK!" cried Brother Monster.

"AAAAAAAAAAAAA

shrieked all the monster aunts
and uncles and all the many
horrible monster cousins.

That perfect little baby monster . . .

was smiling!

To Vanessa, for the vital spark
J. H.

For Audrey
J. L.-S.

Text copyright © 2001 by Judy Hindley
Illustrations copyright © 2001 by Jonathan Lycett-Smith

All rights reserved.

First U.S. edition 2001

Library of Congress Cataloging-in-Publication Data

Hindley, Judy.
The perfect little monster / by Judy Hindley ; illustrated by Jonathan Lycett-Smith. – 1st U.S. ed.
p.   cm.
Summary: A baby monster does all the right things to make his family proud – until his first birthday party.
ISBN 0-7636-0902-1 (hardcover). – ISBN 0-7636-0903-X (paperback)
[1. Monsters – Fiction. 2. Babies – Fiction.] I. Lycett-Smith, Jonathan, ill. II. Title.
PZ7.H5696 Pe2001   [E] – dc21   99-058256

10 9 8 7 6 5 4 3 2 1

Printed in Italy

This book was typeset in Cafeteria.
The illustrations were created in ink and colored in Photoshop.

Candlewick Press
2067 Massachusetts Avenue
Cambridge, Massachusetts 02140